Mister DIVINE, MD

ANDREW MARSHALL, JR.

ISBN: 978-1-63950-257-8 (sc)
ISBN: 978-1-63950-255-4 (e)

This publication contains the opinions and ideas of its author. It is intended to provide helpful and informative material on the subjects addressed in the publication. The author and publisher specifically disclaim all responsibility for any liability, loss, or risk, personal or otherwise, which is incurred as a consequence, directly or indirectly, of the use and application of any of the contents of this book.

Writers Apex

Gateway Towards Success

8063 MADISON AVE #1252
Indianapolis, IN 46227
+13176596889
www.writersapex.com

Dedication/About the Author

This progressive work is being dedicated to the
Historically Black Colleges and Universities (HBCUs),
along with The Fraternities and Sororities comprising
The Divine Nine (9), of which this *Author* is an
Alumnus of, and a member of, respectively.

About the Book

THE Book was pre-conceived as(s) written: Both Metaphor and/or
Simile, and each, if not neither,
Was...wasn't...maybe, maybe KNOT, BOTH simultaneously
(one behind "D" other)....
(C following DISS-CLAIMER):

EYE (Love/Hate) Claims 2-B Disabled every (scary) Time E(WE) Here:
"Want he Screw You?)

Lord (or "LOAD"),
Life (Death) knows EYE AM washed UP with EWE being "down"...
(Seriously, I AM clowning around like THAT "Jive Clown")....
"But you fed the multitude(s)....(some fool niggers coming back, again)
With Just One Fish ('STICK").
Then, Why does HEAVEN fear...
HELL'S ELONGATED DICK!?!?!?!?!?(this shit can go on forever)?!?!....
(Pardon MY disclaimer, but EYE
AM Poetic ("po' at it")(#1 pissed on M-E, got to do #2....
(after EWE, My "Deer")....
(imagine being at a deer's resurrection (CREMATION),
And being forced to ask: "Now, Dew EWE C That...
Goddamn Light?...(sounds like LAMB Chops 2 M-E)....
(Let THE niggers say, "Devil, EYE gonna TELL (TALE)...
Break me off a BIG PEACE of the "Vine-owed" (wine before the ferment)
Little WHALE...

Echo:
Who said: "DAY kneaded a BLACK KIDNEY"?
EWE keeps US high, drunk and Broke,
So WE don't have to pay THE DEVIL for
BEING....NO WITNESS?...Get thefuck in hear, N("word")...
(The END for NOW! But EYE Will C EWE Neck time..)
Willing to FLOOD MY LOVE to HELL,
Cause Heaven got2 many BEACHES....

Contents

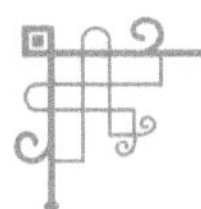

Foolery

Love is like the Snowflakes' melting FLURRY,
A watered-down DEATH that's in No HURRY...

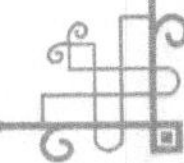

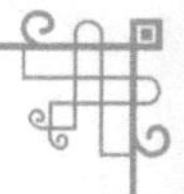

The Black Set Back

"The black set back"
Sounds like a breaking point in an olden but
deadly confirmation,
Where Love might want a "lyricized"
melody in your redemptive song.
It also could be a path to that alarming headache,
Ringing on the outside of the inner ear,
The enchanting chorus harmonizing with damnation:
"Love, Which Death Do You Not Fear?"
But yours is the most multi-rhythmic,
Hell's/Heaven's *Uni-motivational song.*
Know that Black time can be killed,
From violently crawling on the straight and narrow,
Or, just by resting peacefully after being hung.

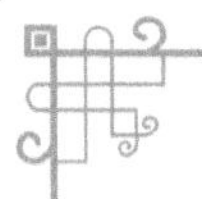

His Purported (Purposely)
Name is "Charles"

Lovely day, aren't these profitable times, Mr. Charlie,

Us agrees for you, "Yes Sir?"

It was a freezing cold,

And none of we didn't outfit "Mrs. Charlie's" prized furs

(don't know his bitches maiden name, okay?)

They don't count out loud your mad money!

Then again,

We know-ed (noted), Yes Sir, that you'se

(you are) Fat (eats the glutton's leftovers).

Yes Sir.

Now, we mind not been talking (thinking) about asking Jesus,

If we could be loaned a little crumb (some) of that.

Everybody did improve for the better,

Since I stayed home, after you left.

Kinda (yeah, kinda) gave you a few more starving -

Cripplings (an empty congregation full),

Just couldn't help my crawling erect, dick-bad self.

(Now, thinking with himself):

After every mysterious hint that I don't really be caring for me,

When I got to control this chilly Black,

Mr. Charles got to being too (two?) empathetic,

Cause He concernly said (don't give one fuck), "My boy,

How is *our stronger* back?

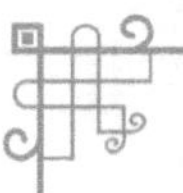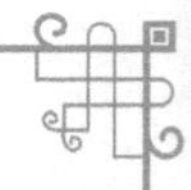

Sightseeing

My Life,
Don't get ahead of me.
What you seem to want,
I might not aspire to be.
"Just live within your compassion,"
As some of your Participants,
Do commandingly pray.
They know that life can always jive,
With any extraordinary day.
Don't get me behind ye, either.
Cause I'm saving this trick for bribing that devil.
Just stay within the commons' area (aerial) view,
So that we shall sightsee and look for forever.

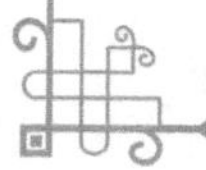

Blessed

I'm not going to do you like that...
Anymore, nor/neither/again.
I have already identify-theft your credit,
To keep the lights from going really dim.
The least little I'm able to do now,
Let you have a partial future,
Where selectivity isn't so grim.

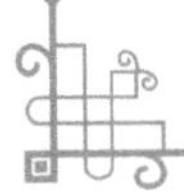

The Eyes of the Black

When I get to the point of the meek's return,
You can bet this fool ain't going to look back.
Cause that "pillar of salt," is the only solution,
For blue wounds delivered to a wounded black.

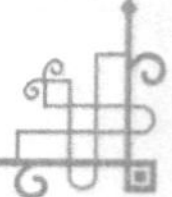

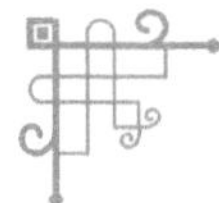

Turning Point

A turning point is before you had been pushed down,
After being forced to come all the way to back around,
To the point where you start with another fresh frown.
The turning point is not unlike a repulsive dissimilation,
A life that's always never lived dying above underground.

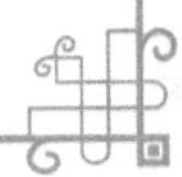

Returning, My Love?

You did not have to doubt or die,
Just to prove your eternal love of me.
Beaten was my heart, but still alive,
in the beyond, post dead, and free.
I was never guilty of any accuser's crime,
Yet, convicted, and a feverish scared.
I, too, carry the weight of the world,
But, before there was truth in you,
There was no reciprocity in *love*...

Two Faces

Sometimes,
Each minute creeps and crawls,
Then, mitigate a march to a crippling walk.
Extremely loquacious,
But never in earnest wishes to talk.
Eats your heart like the glutton who paces,
Then demands a second helping,
When disguised in one of its two faces.

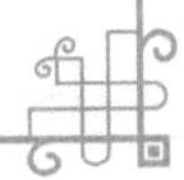

Rouse

I already knew that I had the truth in me,
But had to lure the suppressed in me out.
Had not I been misinformed on my history,
I would not have benefited from the doubt.

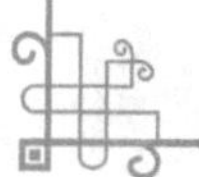

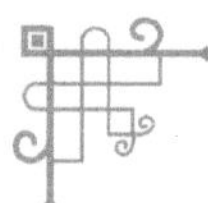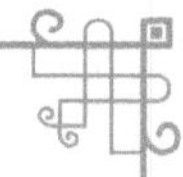

Nobody Times
One Hundred Times a Zero

That's like going to nowhere,
So far, far, far and away.
That's like been left over from,
Your predecessor's deliverance day.
From zero to a multitude of zeros,
With everything defining in between.
But that's not unlike the ghostly days,
Who lives visibly in each and every dream.

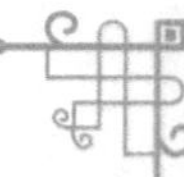

At Seven and
Eleven O'Clocks

Sweeten the pot,
Then parlay the bottom.
The grass appears greener,
Where planted seeds weren't rotten.
Even the score,
Then tie the knot with heaven.
Dust can't rise at midnight,
Until alarming (arming) the clock,
We may check on time
At seven and, then again, at eleven.

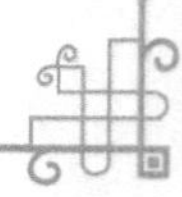

Bliss

You took the love right out of my mouth,
That's where I built your castle.
My words, my truth,
Your friend.
My mouth is what makes love grin.
My mouth houses the tongue's sweetest kiss.
My mouth speaks to the heart of my soul,
Like a kiss from my heart,
Hand holding,
And taking love on one of its strolls.

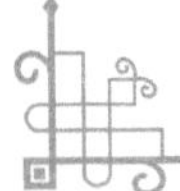

A Caller to Life

Do you take a land line caller's "all or nothing at all"
hook-blowings,
Without known identification?
Who has *called* you without ever getting a tone?
Those desperation callers?
Their mobility in life is immoral, at best!
And should the caller get dropped,
Who should first call the other's a Black...?
Under a protesting scream?
I hear that the towers record your vicinity,
With respect to who was closest to the crime.
Give me the prehistoric pay phone,
That used to waste only your last dime.
Life is unfair,
In that you are still the sum of all that you did not get.
But when you really want to piss off life,
Recall that Bitch's/Bastard's re-collections.

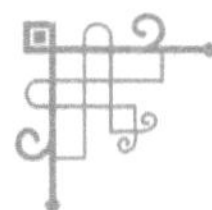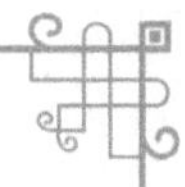

Live Alone

Who doesn't want you to live longer,
Over yonder,
Above the sycamore (either "sic" "sick" or *MORE*) tree,
Where you get to hang with forever,
And let your dead leaves drop,
Beneath my dust-dried, wet-stomping-feet

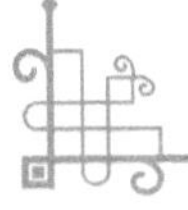

Exception

"All three of them double-teamed on me,
So, I did not withstand much of a chance,
In a spiritless fight to the end of blue sea,
Saving deaths whose rigor mortis' dance."

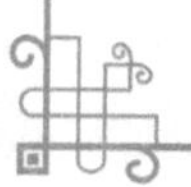

To the Dark Pastel Leeches
(or "Burdensome")

They might act blind,
And envy is as disabling as being a racist can be.
Because they will suction down,
Anything that their eyes cannot stand to see.

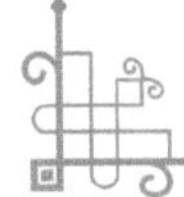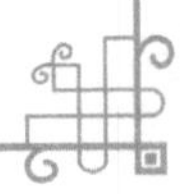

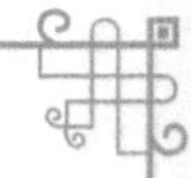

"Set Protesting Free"!!!
(my "Signature")

Protesting
is the same as inheriting *Thee*,
saving that protesting is dead.

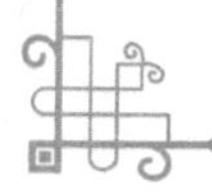
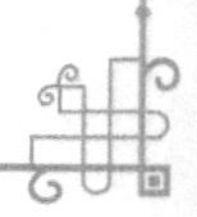

Rearranging My Horns

"I once could see but now I am blind."
Nothing less than the times of the sign.
The wined-down water has a river flow,
(Fast songs I sing while still dancing slow)

The shelf life of love's broken promises"....

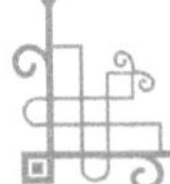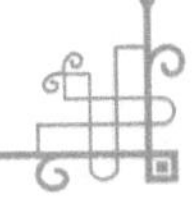

Prospective (Oxymorons And Their Nakedly Dressed Counterparts)

Your most recent distant past,
Had not occurred a multi-second ago.
That's why time got away from backtracking with hell,
And sped up to a pace that isn't as fast as their USUAL -
Slow....

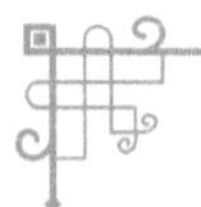

The Wall's Writings on The Fly

See what the walls have written?!
The walls ain't no goddamn joke!?
(TAKE-A-TOTE)!!!
What if the wall could be a wall on the "fly"?
Shall I not do or will I die?
What if the wall had to crawl?
Do maggots have a different incubation period for its shifting hills?
To rest forever in Paradise? How does the inseminated death feel?
What if God's *mooner* wasn't (D) Light?
Would so YESTERDAY see in their darkness,
Given that Candle's propensity for blowings out
Any evidence of THAT Hitchhiker who was drinking
Drunk Juice on the road to Heaven,
Stumbling all alone on Love's sinful plight....

Let That Lifer Go Free

SomeBODY,
Teach me how to talk back to *THE man!*
("Mysteriouly-Absent-Nigger")
Sitting here with my alter-ego-N,
While praying God doesn't PULL
my Trigger...

To/From Whom
The Pulpit Re-Lies

"Raise Your hands if you are building a New Church,
THIS DAY"!!!
But for the pew-stirrers you'd fish for GOLDEN perch,
PER SE....

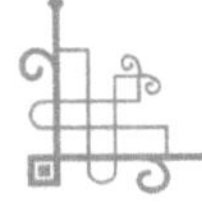

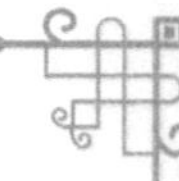

Let's Split The Fangs
(Tab/Bill)

Let's split the fangs,
For I am an Apple, 2.
Let's split the *FANGS*,
Defanging the snake
POISON!!!

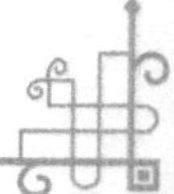

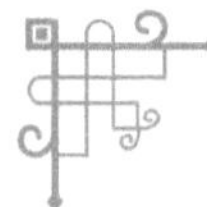

The SUN is Set on Shining

When the SUN sets, I want to be in my *Leather Sweatsuit,*
Watching blood flow from their veins, pinching last nerves,
Acting like the uptown Clown....I want the SUN to rise again.
Then, I want to say to the *SUN:" AMEN, DARKNESS...w/GRIN!!!*

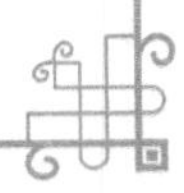

E-Y-E-See Sore

Seen death, and death saw me.
Death said, "Living Sets Life Free"!
Peeped death while dying looking,
(If a traveller did his own booking...)

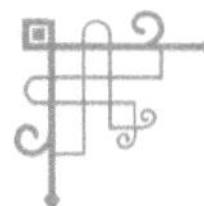

And Me Too

You have everything inside of you,
And you want me to die the death,2.
You are such a dead-penalty- cause:
Love's smart-money, thieving devils,
That even *THAT Death* won't pursue....

Action, Then Mirrored

I wish I weren't from the top shelf,
Of that bottomless pit,
Then I would not have to live,
Always forgiving rehearsed shit.

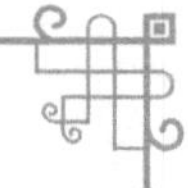

Tipsy

If love is blind,
Then why *did* trouble keep bumping into me?
"Because love isn't blind,
Like that unsighted lover one can only blindly
NEVER see"!

The Publisher (or "You Couldn't be an Editorial, Too"?!)

When you can write your book,
While, simultaneously,
Trying not to settle for newly, rehashed, and rarely young
ancient shit,
Or,
When you learn how to end a fight,
Even when "God" started it in the beginning.

Let's Reveal Love's
Better Secrets

Let's reveal the secret of love's most favorable place to hide.
The first place to look is where love keeps its stubborn pride.
This revelation is more or less where innocence hearts play,
Before the introduction to love's deserted *EMPTY* hideaway.

Let's discuss some places love, habitually, pretends to GO.
Love doesn't always keep love that washes up to its Shore.
Love drinks from the chalet of sweet blessings SO DIVINE:
The Matchmaker That ignites eternity's HEART with MINE!

Dimpled

Who told you that you were not Cute?
Did they *Snort* like a dead-blind-mute?
Were they there for Love's Braille Sign?
Is it *THEIR Business*, Or just NOT MINE?

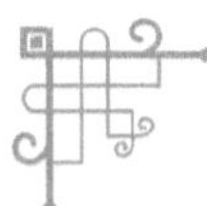
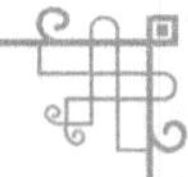

Burden

After lifting your lighter burdens,
Don't leave your strength behind.
Burdens are *Successfully Heavier,*
The longer the weary must *GRIND....*

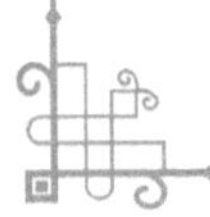

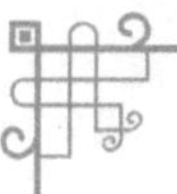

Staggerlees

Though seeing is believing,
What the blind didn't see!
Ask another blind,
One who is not tripping over me.
Though disbelieving is hindsight,

The Blues Book of De-Parted Ways

Can I look?
The things YOU hide....
If WE the CROOK,
AGAIN, *the US has* lied.
May I lay time on its back,
Page by page?
I did read ("red") something
Kind-like and Kindred to that.
May I picture colored love,
Without the disparaging frowns,
Not knowing to look up,
While, simultaneously,
Bending down?

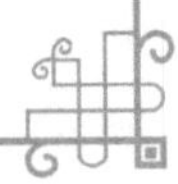

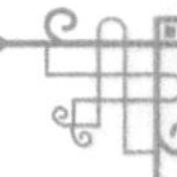

Helper, Do You Not Love Your Helpers (The Early Fall)

Love me before
MY early Summer,
Kiss my lips asunder.
Project my breeze,
Before the tardiness of
The Early Fall.
Love me like there is
No shortage of love,
Like love is gluttonous,
Having devoured more than *ENOUGH*
Love from US *ALL*....

Cell "C" or Fahrenheit "C" Love

Cell "C" Love or Fahrenheit "C"?
(One N is too many less Ns for Me)
Interpreting The NinterruptingN:
Celsius is to Fahrenheit
What godly Low is to damned Down.
Seeing all that gold, to the blind
Is akin to drinking on well water
After BEING salt-watered-down.

Sugar/Salt (That Child's Broke, ALL of His Whine Bottles Done, Gone EMPTY!?)

Before he was a talking/walking *supt. STAR,*
LOVE had his fingers pointing at *THE* MOON.
Don't mention that crippling, baby-TODDLER,
A *Chariot swinging with* empty water bottles...

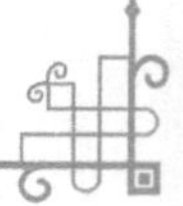

Not Without Standing
Away From The Hands

I'm not suggesting that you will not sit before God,
Nor throw stones at the Judgement's baby grands.
Like all ceremonies that celebrate, ceremoniously,
Now the climbers ropes are betting on dead hands.

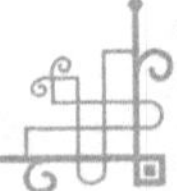

False Setters
(Sun, Is That You?)

I'm not giving you any more of these -
Baby-making songs.
You make the Sun screened,
From her thongs.
Naked that Song,
Dressed to sway.
My Song can not set,
'Til after the moon comes,
Out of its clouds for a "Free for All",
Foreplay.

God Did Not Make Any Mistakes, Mistakenly

God did not make any everlasting mistakes,
So, the devil must've mistaken-*sleep/awake:*
So meek and beautiful We're envied-Indeed;
Let Death inherit This Hell, *Mister Con-Seed....*

Crawling A Long....
Lord, so glad to be walking again!?
And the Lord said: "...how you been
Moving down the road with *good sin*?"
Lest WE come back and *DO* it again!?

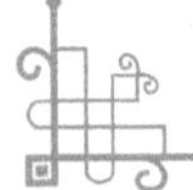

Downtown

How can a soul be deprived and not declared dead?
Does Sunday's best hustling maggot live death-fed?
Can the body wither away 'til it chokes and drowns?
Did you rent hell's worst lot in your other downtown?

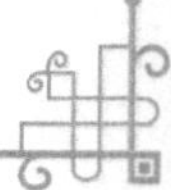

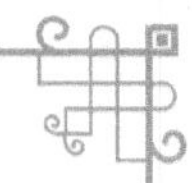

Like That Revere Rider?
(or "How Fast Was You Going to be Gone, Before Passing Back Out?")

When Y'all first met "M-E":
You knew not that You needed 1 *head-doctor-doctorings*.
This is soon to be re-approaching -
Before-Medicalogically-Fitting.
This due to a lesser indictment,
of how much of the inspired Word wasn't subject to subjugation.
While I'm under the caring of the Psycho-Therapeutic-Caregivers.
Additionals from my pre-posting of a aesthetic dislikings,
Should not have been factoring in the fact that:
You are now (in-temporarily) not under the *Fool's* licensing.

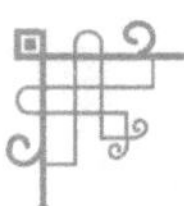

Stationary

She said, Knight,
How come you didn't write back
to me, over the tears,
every day, through the rainy years?

He said, Shiny,
I was eloping with that slow- minded Death,
Procrastinating in the center of hell's Pig Pen,
Slopping for the cropping - NEVER again!!!

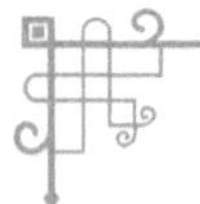

One Stern Lashing

"EWE know that you are going *Niggerly correct,*
To the word "betray" *(B-E-V-E-R-L-Y S-C-A-R-E-D),*
But don't think about turning warm water to cold,
Just wait until you get to see another sunny day!"

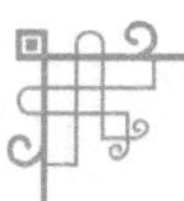

Valley Boy (According 2 God: Three Days In Paradise)

Valley boy?!
Where's Valley Girl?
Is she Still-Stoned-Drunk,
Jacking the world off,
While holding your hand?
When does a boy child become a man?
When does a soft-broken-heart become hard again?
No watered-down-water for me!
Just Heaven's upper hill GIN....

"That Mule couldn't last no more than
Three Days in THIS here PARADISE"

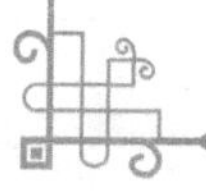

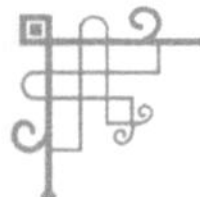

Pleasantries

I really thank you for *that*,
Cause we can use all the help
That one can never seem to get.
"Thank You!" "Thank You!" Thank You!"
For all the love that ain't worth *spit*,
Just always tempted to have me another round of –
The Beggar's Fix.

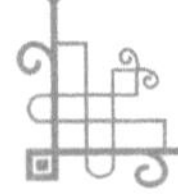

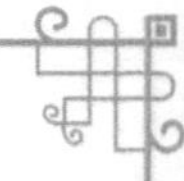

Thee Hourly SUNroom

Leave LOVE a little piece of that *pocket change,*
As you exit (sneak out of) death's *OURly* ROOM.
We are HEAVEN and HELL-BOUND ("arranged"),
Dressed down to be UP with the Bride or Groom!?

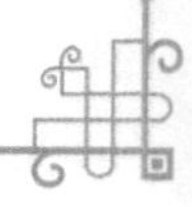

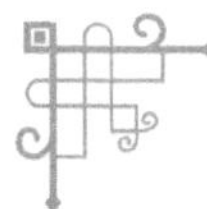

Death, Beg Forgiveness

Death, beg forgiveness
and change your wicked ways.
Unlike the gods who come before you,
you discriminate.

You are like the gluttonous capitalist
whose belly is filled with blood
But cannot quench the gulf of hate salt-water-thirst.

The roads to hell pass through your gates,
and you pave the way an asphalted salvation:
Hand-basketed them all with perfected sickness and sin,
and like a monster rejoicing in the annihilation of innocent souls,
YOU grin!

You have so long killed to be loved,
until there is no life in dying for YOUR forgiveness.
A beautiful angel you may have been,
but envy has made you green and molded.

Does the Creator fear the reprobate heart,
or hear the cries of her children before facing death's *DARK*?
Who else but you should inherit this wretched earth
that the UN-fathered have desecrated with
its misdirected ways of multiplying,
After committing, then cursing OUR father
(however hallowed be *thy* names)?

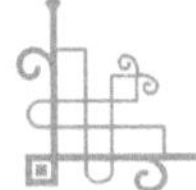

You say, "Man lives only once,
so let him be of good cheer and depart from his wickedness."
But some dying souls truly know that death is an inevitable end,
so they live and celebrate The *Life gone away.*

What arrogance that you should hold time in contempt,
while you contemplate asking forgiveness,
still personifying the dead and their pompous, predestined ways?

Yours like hers is the epitaph of Love's fall:
"Sterility Hath Killed Us All"!
Death, beg forgiveness
and change your evil ways!!!

Contents

Profanely Insane/"GNP" ("Gross NiggerS Productions")
(Subversives in The Blue Book)

Smart Money

Don't worry about or shitting about
Shit you can't do shit about.
That's like trying to speed up that slow hand (finger)
On the trigger (clock).
Even kinda, sorta like snow melting away in the early dark
sunlight (gonna happen!),
Or the really smart ones believing that being right is so
Motherfuckingly *bright*.

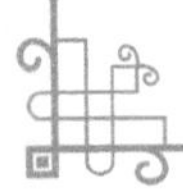
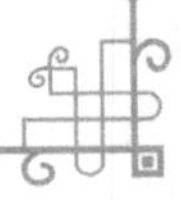

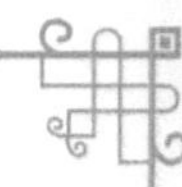

"Blew-Cheese-Bre(a)D"

EYE trained my *high-powered-scope* (B)
rain) on dat lit' bit' blue (black) bird
(COCK!!!)....
Hating crazy-foolish-numb-niggers
("bloodpeckers") the ways *OUI (nous) do,*
I (*me diss tyme*) TOLD (asked) *LOVE*: "How does reciprocity
(*Bartering*) feel?"
Why (k)not invite DEATH ('em) "N" (*words*) *end,* AND take (*T*)
hey BREAD!?
"We ALL shall (*save the baptised*) bruise their fucking,
loquacious *HEAD*"!!!

Lord, Let Me End ("On iT")

Lord, Let Me End ("On iT")
My soul cannot take another ONE of your Jokes.
Hell is so hot, © why the burning SUN pop smoke?
My tears over-floored with cleaning UP Heaven's
DIRTIEST HOUSE (*Death-Alarmining-MANSION*)....
I choke in BATTLE, so give me my own SWORD (*ewe LORD!?*)
DEW EYE HEAR RESERVATION EXPANSION?

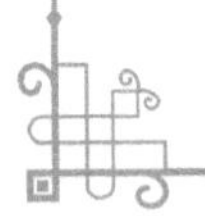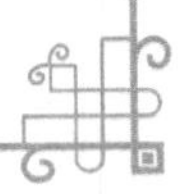

Mona Lisa Looking Smile
(If Only for The Goddamn Camera)

I might be the gods babysitter,
But WE ain't keeping Yo' child.
Can't trust a LOVE's that bitter,
With *Mona-Lisa-Looking Smile...*

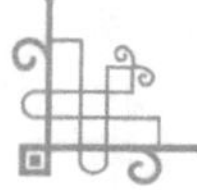

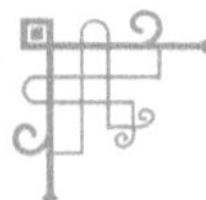

Now, Back to You
(Ghostly)

If you aren't the fuckin' scary,
Then most likely you are his motherfucking "Boo!"
And this is the greatest show of goddamn affection,
Passed on to me, from the Devil,
And...now, forwarded to EWE....

"BAN" ("Bitch-Ass-NiggerS"/ "Bitch-Ass-Nevermine"/ "Bitch-Ass-'Notherfucker")

The white liver spiritual is just a goddamn "ban(D)! Ass, OUI march to shit (dog do! do!) EWE n-words Done (CON-MAN(d) shit....

One Mansion's Dimensions

What is the minimum dimension needed to be a Mansion great?
Can we all fit without being chained and
gagged at the pearly hate?
Do you really want more ways back down
to that Heaven with them?
Would God be the wiser by giving you another set of open eyed?
How dare God raise you high then retire before
"To Tide-ass Heaven, Thee Live"?
And how demanding Hell never gave a damn about how I feel!
(How "you're been re-fucked, Again" feels?)

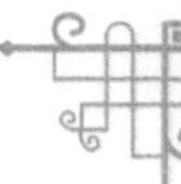

Sweetest? Sweetest? Sweetest?

This is, to haven't been, exactly,
What Heaven yells.
Dumbest-Blindest-Escavatingest!
And the tastiest in Hell wants a -
Darken(est)-Chocolate(ing)-Girl!
"Go Fuck-UP a-World"!!!

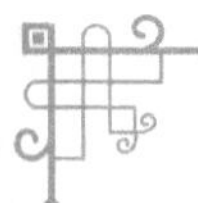

Contemplation

I'm still trying to figure out,
why that goddam chariot didn't swing lower.
We had to be reaching for it, High.
If a chariot (carrot) could truly swing,
Everyone would catch it on the fly.
That chariot must've been fucking blind,
After all the help with descending,
We were only homing the Brave.
Now they're claiming the Bitch as co-Pilots,
Ascended,
Before giving a goddamn "you are really been fucked now,
Contemptuous Wave."

Some Crazy Shit

Are you going crazy "over the shit?"
Behind the shit?
Either way,
You got to take out some "shit."
But be careful,
You wouldn't want the opposition calling you
A "smelly bastard!"
The children say it best:
"You smell like shit,
Cause you *is/ain't* shit..."
Shitty behavior?
But you shouldn't go crazy over the shit,
Behind the shit,
Or about the shit.
However, I am going to have a shit,
Before I deal with mo' shit.

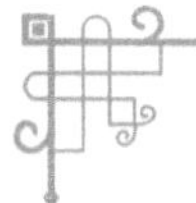

Above My Wounded Knees

I do whatever the fuck I don't wait to get done,
To get undone,
Whenever I can, fuck! If I can.
A life like this I never intended for me.
Now, this I "do not" understand.
Say when you say "goodbye,"
Don't want to hear weeping souls cry.
Not but One Nigger better not sit down,
So, that I don't have to rollover and push away cupping hands.
Just tell the thunder about the rain.
Tell the sun that dark bright days were a pain.
Tell a loser who is now insane,
You had about a "little" less gain.
And if this means that a more majority of you didn't cry,
Then you must've lived along, pushing on 'head to die.
I finally cured my life of trying to please.
Even poured love on an incurable disease.
Once or twice (smoking buddies),
Boldly told that devil, it will be -
"Do or die"?
Then bullshitted with God,
When giving eternity a try.
I still owe debts,
I can never repay.
Open-eyed chases at love,
Gone past unforgivable astray.

I have done more than all that I do not know;
Got battle scars I flaunt for show.
I might choose to die "Proof Proud" in an abandoned mortuary,
Although the idea of not having lived,
Is just as scary.
In Repentance Theology,
I have lived my life above the bended knees.
And not that I'm passing for Judgment Day,
But I will not die until Heaven finds our lost keys.

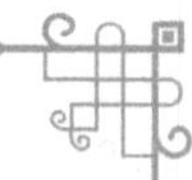

I Come Around to the Back Around

We go to the back, around,
Then, you lay the fuck down,
In the background
Until we don't speak,
Not even late next week,
After you come down with
Some of your coldest frowns.

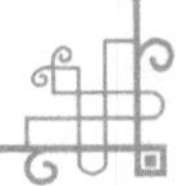

An Urn-Wrap Around

EYE knew that you were planning to Fuck ME *UP*,
When you poured SALT in my eyes for going BACK!
I knew that EWE was Heaven's premature *NEWBIE*,
Cutting the ceremonial umbilical cord if cock's black!!!

Even After God was Notified of My Returning

Didn't do all of that goddamn praying,
to one day be this fucking Nigger poor.
You have salted my plethora-addicted wounds,
With hypertension from shitty swine manure.
Now, you've made my life eternally sunny Black.
With revered respect to Merciful God,
I've already dis-repossessed -
both of them assholes back.

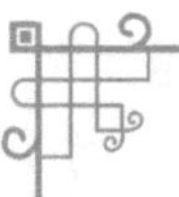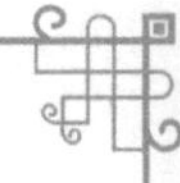

Lyme

There is none rectoanal-diseased,
Who isn't a pain in the ass *sleeves*.

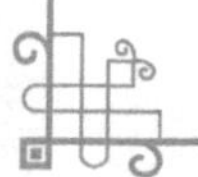

Immunity (What More or Less Must The Same Sinner Do?)

You can't grant immunity,
Against your own having been god-damned,
Only self.
"immunity" implies that you must be truthful about
The ones who got fucked,
And, justifiably, in totality,
Sold out for that watered-up *pee...*

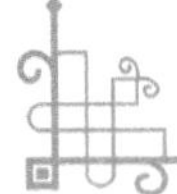

Best That The Cock Crewed

You already got one of his strikeouts against...,
Now what? You want to give the apple pie back?
Since I've gotten to know you better
(lived with you, much too long),
You must be that re-lying gift,
from the dark lily whites to the courage-stricken Black.
Then what are you going to do,
If he never pitches to you, or even let you roll it slow?
Take another goddamn walk,
Then question the loser's score?
Listen, pretty knees,
Niggers ain't gon be like liking to clean no fishy-ass crow.
"So, let me tell you what the fuck I'd do,
For saying, I'm the anti-decibel whisper from
the throne beneath you below.
I'd bet it all on you and all are more than nothing a'tall,
But more of your favorite tasty carnage,
on a scale of numbers from don't want no
trouble to nothing, including zero.
Don't want no trouble,
But your gluttonous asses will go crippling
in wrap around straight lines,
if you knew your "drain" Man was willing to sell you another
"heaping helping" of that deadly-delicious white crow.

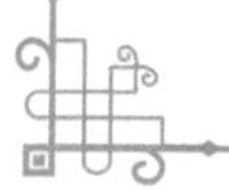

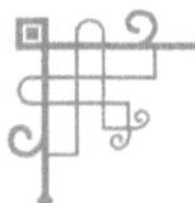

Mourning Knee-Grow(N)

Of Course, You Know Whose Abjection,
Prospectively, is Getting a Kick
("Act Like You Are Not Going to Have
Already Been Feeding the Fed)

Every bully that I have not, yet, realistically,
Never, un-truly, known,
(And cannot, credibly, desist-my-own (okay, to "disown"),
Have kicked a circle ("circus"?) in my "retangular" ass (the
three sides of true:
The Beginning, The Ending, And Niggers-Blue),.
Now, I get to be the bullied,
At Last.
"Mothersfuckers took Your god...(damn! car....
And your stationary ass ran out of gas (it's just a fart!).
Yeah, "Niceties" makes for being second closest behind the first,
"At Last"!

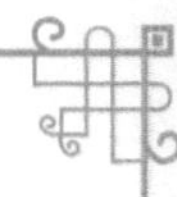

When Wimp Pimps Get Diss-Robe(d)

This ain't no trickster shit,
My trickin' bitch.
You are the fuck trick,
That makes a snitch-lusting-hitch,
Get THE pussies C-sections-stitched.

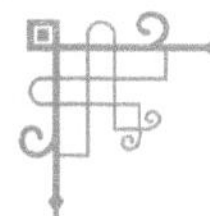

A Slice of That Light Bread and A Little BIG-Mouth Bass Sandwiched

I WASN'T FREE TO STOP OVER FIRST!
Then, you best be last re-moved.
This *HOOD* is a sanctuary,
Wrong-Ns be out of their *lusting* groove.
From the first to the second to THIRD,
Y'ALL *believe as if* YOU were the first to be here first,
How *fucking* (no other ways to do it) ABSURD.
WELL, WE was hurriedly *HOME*, too.
Now, to prove US wrong, this what your figures can't DO:
"The first of the first isn't the first of the last.
And the last to be first will go up FIRST CLASS.
WE ALL shall share the *BREADY-BREAD-BRED*,
Along with a PIECE of that (rockfish/striped) BASS!!!

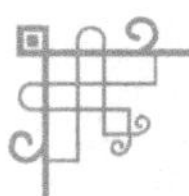

Magazine Feeders
("MFs")

I am not cursed,
But I do swear:
Those harpooning MFs
Couldn't just stare.
Had to "William Tell"
Love's peace arrow,
Now, go and *DUCK YOURSELF,*"
Your "aspis" is a myth *NARROW.*

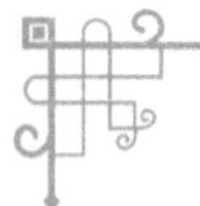

The SUN Always Shining on Yo' Back Will Make You White Hot with Blue Breath

Whether the sun fucks me on my back,

Or say, fuck your back,

I am being semem-dried,

Been fucked *BURNED* for fun.

Of all people,

Why would my knees put on me -

The posterizing posture of a pun?

What a fuck1?

Now, the children are heat-stroke-driven,

For a contaging,

Telling the other *late* runners: *"Got Your Luck"*!

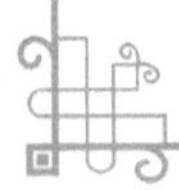

Magical

The greatest trick of this life is to make pretend that
It is real!?
But with a lightning faster than death,
He strikes down civil rights bills.
The devil has his "Adams" who'd swear to always given
But never undertaking.
These are those bastards who eat the apples
Of souls that must bite the venomous snakes.
It is written,
"They can't fool Me, if it were not for the
impossible" (paraphrasing).
When it's cold inside, you kill them from the "tropical"
(just in case others want to lay claim to your inheritance).
Still, that motherfucker wants the world to
think that you aren't real (stay young!),
While charging you with homicide after each of you he's killed.
Don't let them upset your love for him with
your forgiveness of perfect hate,
He has already created mountain falls of baby black tears.
Actually, that thang ain't real...
With the exception for the heaping of a death grip.
Whenever he is feeling good the whole wide world,
Goddam! Why did they know?
But when you want a true taste of his freedom:
Incarcerate the soul! *Don't want to be slower than slow.*

Contents

Mrs. Blues' Child
Insurmountable Incidentals

MY laboring made Wall Street what she wasn't,
Until today.
But when hate took birth,
My death turned towards gray.
I've crawled countless miles,
While pulling love out of sin.
Hadn't even forgiven my enemy,
Before, like a vision, he was all up in my mirror, again.
I've walked in everybody's shoes,
Sometimes marathons,
In the sun, now,
In a long sleeved, black and heavy-leather jacket.
But before I done went on ahead and die retire,
I dream of winning lottery numbers,
Which is not oddly good, but beats being
in those loser's brackets.

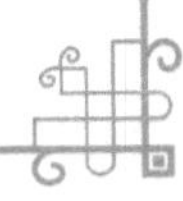

I'm The Champ-Pain!! Why Won't God Give Me Another Title Fight

If lit' bit' "J" wants to fight me (and a fair fight
against *Biological Municipalities isn't wrong)*,
But, unlike EWE, I'm listening for MY Ancestors
to say: *"Bring That dark-Black Ass Home"!!*

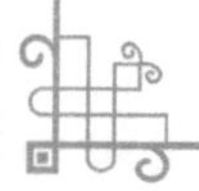

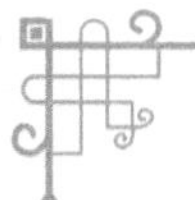

Of Sight I Am Relieved

"If seeing is believing,"
What does the *blinded* see?
Can they trust the faith in their belief?
Am I at all trusting of the Blind?
I hope that which I have not seen,
Yet to be believed,
Conferred.
Much unlike the sightful blind,
I can see the darkness in the enlightenment,
After being relieved.

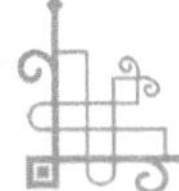

"Say Uncle, Nephew"!
("Ewe Ain't My Father's Brother"!)

"Cry Baby"!
Your Mother!
(Isn't hard to tell who's doing all the "talking" here.)
Anyway...
My Mammie wasn't crying' (had to leave off the hard "g" in
the end);
She was "weeping"!
"Weepin'"?
Well, then,
Betcha Yo' Nightmares ain't never truly "sleeping."

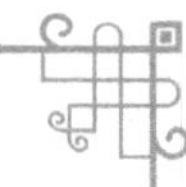

Paraphrasing
("Pair O' Phrases")

I tried using that line about: "You can't afford to fire me,
Cause *love* been workin' it for free."
Let me tell you! This does the work,
But, Y'all (Saint-less, Least-Sinners) still got to get
Yo' AfricanoAfrogelling-Acting (AAA).
(Some Niggers be thinking they haven't been left ("on the left")
On that self-darkening, and concrete-desert-
dismemberment, lowered away}.
You cannot not afford to not bring about the demises.
Who else in hell is willing to show the light
on "thus" (that's "thee" plus "us").
(And who else but one of us, blameless, shall
not end each's beginning here?)
And you can't let me go?
It is Creation's blood that will over-crowd ("flood") Heaven!
This I know,
Cause the 'Bilical Cord tells me so.
(Now, I know what they mean when that "Henn/Gin" kicks...
"end")

Echo:
I don't say this loud,
But, my *Job* got "fired."

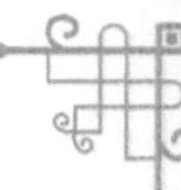

Look Upon Me and Rebuke
Just Not Only The Lust

Now that you have seen my nakedness,
Could you still love me with my blinders on?
What if I were fully un-aware of shameless, innocent nudity,
Would the heart not beat to a less satiable wrong?
Let me not make you strip my soul of the tenderness,
Reducing the non-believer to blowing his last kiss towards wishing.
My fermented juices run to you like a new religion,
Having no damnation for homelessness, housing no inhibitions.

I'm a Live Brother, Child Baby

They don't just bury the dead,

They scurry the scared.

And I was alive,

(prior to this switch).

Bitch!

Only the doctoring had clue,

The baby does not die - dead:

All wrapped up in his closing fist.

If I were not dead,

Would I be tempted, in our united blood, to write this?:

All rats don't dislike cheese.

Some rodents suffer the rabid disease.

Itching and scratching where there should be no itch.

If you weren't a dog,

You still can't be my bitch.

And it does not begin here.

Your mamas fucked our daddies,

Dear.

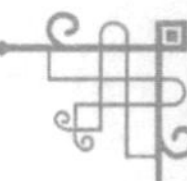

The Charm of Slum's Harm to Calm

Let them roaches ride,
And head-starters:
"Butter and/or Cream"?
Double-dipping like this,
Makes you a little too short,
To be a bringin' ups' downs, backing into that dream.
(If you had one, too,
You be been knowing,
Somebody talks, sorrowfully, 'bout behind a screw:)
A screw must be *losing* ("losting"),
Like your mirrors got the nervous,
Chastising all of y'all look-alike - Yous.
Instead of beating their hearts in thunderous prosecution,
They "Rise" ("raised") up to the dissitement bequeathed the blind,
"Sighted Fool"!

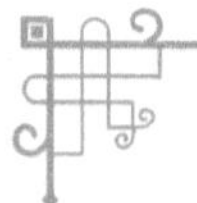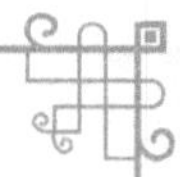

A Good Woman is Not Plastic

A good woman may also be a doll-like plastic,
And still flex her muscles like they aren't elastic.
After accusing your man of doing much wrong,
You continue hanging around to make him groan.
If a man is going to be loved unconditionally true,
He needs an unbiased negotiator to combat you.
Whereby all good women are often treated bad,
Their plastic doll's lust is so unapologetically *mad*.

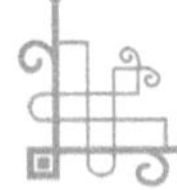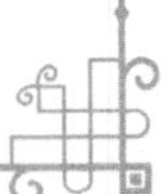

He and His She Love

He?
He is a once god-fearing,
Disenfranchised,
Would die to live free,
Like an unshackled Man.
And She?
She loves him with all the strength,
Love can lift up,
with a broken-hearted hand.

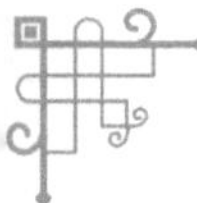

Forever Begins Again, Today

Don't look now,
But love is coming your way.
Stop looking back!
The causes for that occurred during a hurried stay.
You may look ahead,
But cautiously,
I Pray.
While heaven is the destination,
Forever begins again, today.

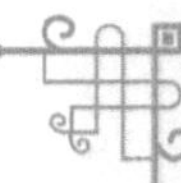

A Dove's un-Hatchings

Let's not be physically,
Intimate,
Before moving each to mental hate.
Let's keep our hearts
Fully dressed,
And do propose a most chastely,
"Dining Date!"

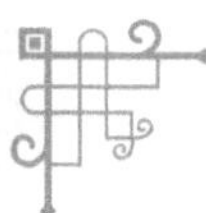

Do Scratch That

My love that won't die,
Without a heavenly collapse.
Do scratch "that."
"My heart is as broken as a broke forgiver,
Who can't buy love that will save from attack....

Who? And Who is You?

That works for the dumb aspirers (and "Asses").
(If you could see, you would be hearing the grin of a whip
(*Whipping*).
But all of this has passed passe as well,
Because you have been doing light work for them.
However lucky for you,
Your future is a bit' anorexically,
Grim.

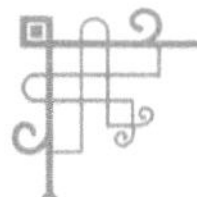

The Other Envy

You wouldn't envy such a Beautiful Angel,
if you weren't locked out of the darker skin.
You wouldn't be so ugly and so unattractive
to love's natural colors that make *ENVY SIN*....

"Play D and get C and F, 2"

Taste the swine after they swallow *its* cud!?
Then add no specks of that peckered MUD!...
(While SALT gleams for your 4-ever-darkness,
Africa's Love is Reincarnation taking *Her rest*....

Good Morning

"Good *Mourning*, Good Niggers,
Time to get your Lazy asses up.
You were lively last night
When you wanted to fuck, fuck fuck."

It's like your Brother had said,
"Now cunt is good and that's no jive,
but you got to swim not fuck
to stay alive."

Like the man said,
Get your *Colorful* asses up,
Every addicted 20 million of you.
Your numbers haven't changed
Since you were blackened in '62.

Wars are waging strong:
The coloreds versus the anti-blacks.
When you see the white on their eyes,
Aren't for rolling back.

Good Afternoon, Niggers,
You Dearly Beloved.
No dancing in these dead-ends-streets....

Indian Head Penny

I also lost my found Indian Head Penny,
Minus the roaming Buffalo.
Back then,
The "Wild West" was really "Serially Slow" (original).
I exclaimed, "No Buffalo!?"
And the *"delighted" "green devil"* said "(multiple emphases"),
You too, black-ass, Indian-loving, nigger-looking tree,
And your mamma is from "Africa," (too
many compliments, for you too?)
Cause within your indelibly decaying blue blood,
"Me Still Can See in Only One Hateful Dead Shade of Red,
White, Blue HATE!"

Reception

I'm now and forever receptive to anything
Love hasn't already (*loquaciously*) said,
But still elect to say *MY SAY!*
Because I rendered your decision,
From Justice,
In more of a less –
Judicial way.

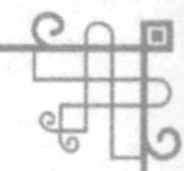

The Mirror That is Filled with a Reflection of Mutual Love

Is life being as lovely to you,
As you have been a tenant?
Did love break your heart,
While retaining your deposit,
Making LOVE a *rent hoarder?!*

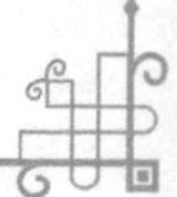

Love and Heaven

Love and heaven has always been married
To one and the other's single-minded twin.
While love just might assassinate the heart,
Heaven is the deadliest sniper 2 BEFRIEND!

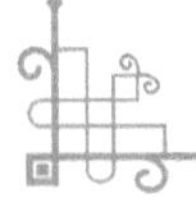

Sentencing Eyes

I've seen men lynched,
Then given a life of imprisonment,
For refusing to die past their time.
I know people who murder humans right,
And they are rewarded all of the heavens,
Combined!

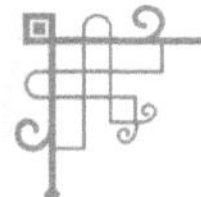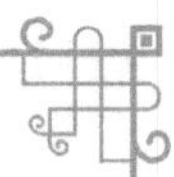

Love Has Not The Time to Watch

You are the taste for my love,
And I love the way love tastes.
My love is running true deep;
My heart has entered the race.

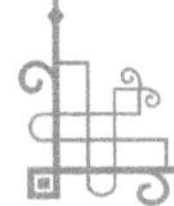

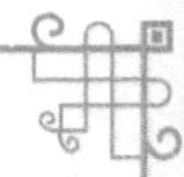

Window Shopping and Still Looking to Buy a Goodbye

You once loved the denotation – "simultaneously,"
So, now you owe hell,
Because they are both multi-tasking,
And all are insanely insane, crazy excessively,
Freed away from charging time.
Before, "My, how they have grown,"
The minds were idling very well,
And, also, they were caught looking at a fine time....

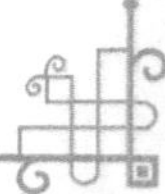

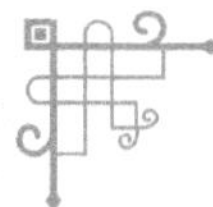

Allegiance

"I don't have no allegiance to you,"
Cause didn't know where to find my (*submission papers*).
I, bluntly, rolled them into yonder,
Where heaven smells its spilled vapor.

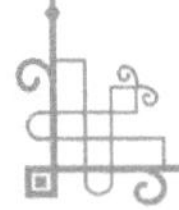

Ahead of Me

Don't get Ye ahead of me,
Because I am not the "me" of whom you should be following
Through the wilderness of an unfamiliar,
Yet,
You already know what is expecting to come,
Reality.
But to make a short road long,
Gone!

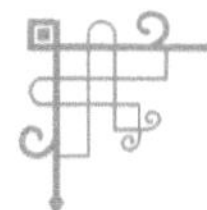

Sum Times Time Does Knot
Knows With Whom Time
Spent Time's Last Time

Sometimes time moves slow...........
Sometimes time went FAST!
Fast Times go much FASTER
Then slow times *gone* SLOW!
Neck Time when I do MY Time,
Time won't mean Shit to *TIME*...
(TIME?! Time!? time!...Time2GO....

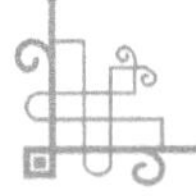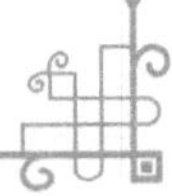

Being The Last 2 Pass Makes Your Green Light Read, White And W/O Hue

Oh Black (K)nights,
Them BLUE lights
Shall Always...
SHINE on Y-O-U!!!

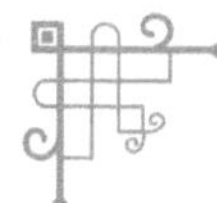

My Soul's Preoccupation

My soul's preoccupied with the lovelier things in *You*,
Like dreaming whether love will pay *the price of True*.
My heart is leaving rose petals along the road *to gold*,
Don't make me the carrier for the lowest bidder's load!
Send one up, or come down to sign my heart's repent -
Bequeath to US a heaven that craves love's *free scent*.

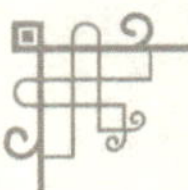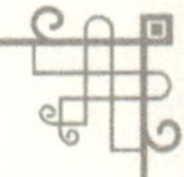

As if Love Hasn't Already Gone There

LOVE must be coming from HELL?!
I cannot see The Light, save SMELL...

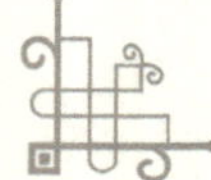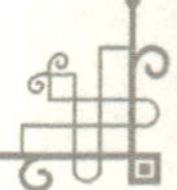

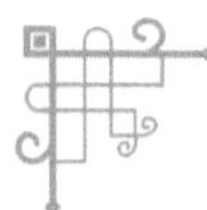

My Heart Hasn't
Been Grounded

My prison looks like a little Mansion,
All closed-captioned, sound-proof,
To the "non" insomnia,
Disturbing the sleeplessness in internalizing the intermittence.
(There is no difference in the difference
being the same indifference).
Cheer Yourselves!
No greater bullshit shall we never overcome following.
"My hearts haven't been forever such a *grounder*,"
But you cannot never disinherit,
The searches and findings of the Founder.

Piss

What's the Weather Like in the Passing?...Give You Buttered
Milk on My Panties Cake (or "Let to Live Without the Differences")
(or "This ain't That Goddamn Better Than
The One I'm Throwing Back to Me")

Just break the partnership,
And we shall find another mine.
Embrace me with my freedom (another's free verse),
And, epidemiologically speaking,
We feel YOUR free waters on the US's spineless spine.

Pee

Thirsty Tree...I Play with You, Cause You Isn't My Friendly, But
if You Don't Know My Types of Blooding, You Will Not Have
Played Yourself Like They Aren't Unlike Me

The cause being:
I hate longer titles speaking not only about my sorrows.
I want to sip fermented wine,
Like a dog pissing on the *thirsty tree.*
I'd skipped Tomorrow,
If I had known that the futures weren't
Inclusive of historical me.
I am the past of love's possessiveness,
Just Me!:
The seller of an ejaculated life
That peed on my life while quenching the thirst of
A dead hanging Tree...

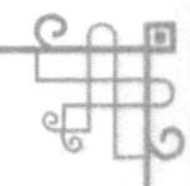

This Is Not My Next Gig
(As If Speaking In Braille Do
Not Require Interpretation)

I haven't been led to be dis-believing that one's next *Job*
Isn't the under-composed,
Disenjoyment that's riddling Your body with cryings,
From never having been loved so good,
Like it wasn't my gig to wanna see *The-Longest-Big*.
We are feeling unlike, Not-Now-LoverBoy,
Do You think I've been gone as long as Y'all?.
But, Somehow,
Inherit the maniac-festation of the delusional.
You didn't think I don't think?
I'm the goddamn Police-Pimp-Pimped.
(I haven't truly *reported* on you, though.)
But even the Senses-Seeking-Brailler,
Will see how it feels to smell the ashes
Of those who do not read unsightly signs:
"They must've known Not that closed, non-working eyes,
Only works for the blind-sighted.".

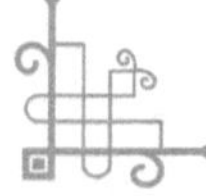

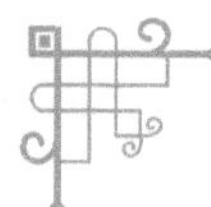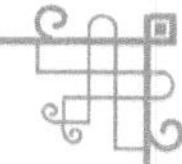

Heaven is Raining
on the Reigning

Heaven is reigning in on the raining,
And the soldiers swords cut like a
Psychopathic-Avenger-Revenging,
The killing of *dead's* years of tears.

Heaven is reigning in on *The Raining,*
And must the Lord hold compassion
For the sobs of the screaming mutes?
Hell cried for love's sorrowful rebuke....

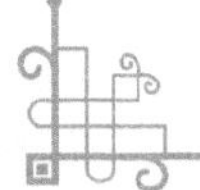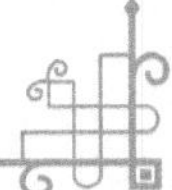

The First Thing You Do in Anybody's Place is Look Down on Compliments

Don't tell me about no gluttons,
When I can't get Nominations for an awarding:
"Me, My Race, and Eye"!
It was Me running around with the *Race*,
The Eye does not lie!
Just ask *that Benedictioning BLIND!*
Love must see that heaven and hell,
Aren't the only two of the same kind.

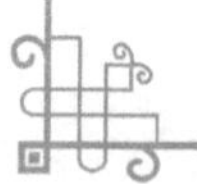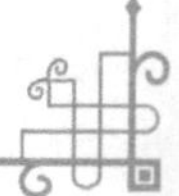

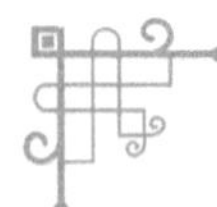

If Anyone is Deserving of a Death's Discount It's the Last Breath That's Been Holding Back

"Too much business have WE given to EWE,
In this greatest motherfucking GULF DIVIDE,
That's why LOVE gives HATE the backSLIDE"?!

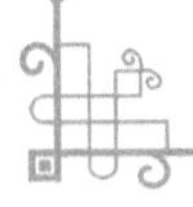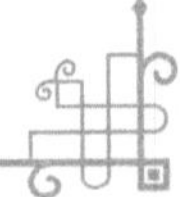

Looking Into My Mirror and Seeing One's Only Deferment

There are just some *four-legged* words I don't use,
Cause I'm not going through the repentance process,
from a fucking homebound, convalescing church.
Shit! I walk with three canes, too.
Although I can take you as you are,
You can't save this man lives with those three letters,
And if you can see another "miracle" betraying the "forgiven,"
Then you should be trying a different
command like "dog" "ass" "git!"
Don't break too many lives with molded bread.
You can slip on dry water,
Just as fast as the dead can throw the first stone.
So, instead of making hell heaven's shame,
Just keep pulling until you get to the rope's end,
Or the face in the mirror's unforgivable sin.

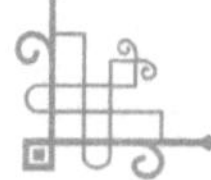

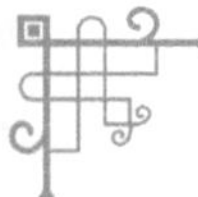

Dropping Dimes

"When there is a critical circumstance,
You may exploit the name of the Lord.
But Life should never spend its DIME,
While bleeding on the weapon, *Sword*!!!

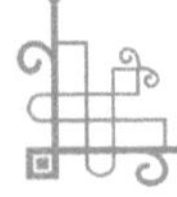

My Dream...

Or, go to sleep in hell's sematary,
And rob dead roses in your souls.

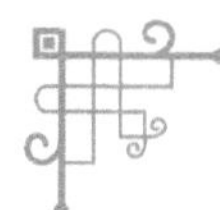

Also, or "Too Much Love and Unselfishness for You to Make True"

Also:
Blown was your love's inheritance,
by wishing upon French Kisses,
Along the Côte d'Azur.
As I now know what should've been my dreams for you,
There I want to live, and take *LIFE's final tour*

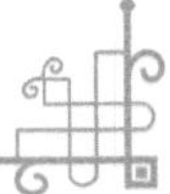

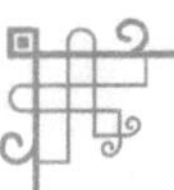

Falsely Alarmed

It's just a get-back for not answering
What sounds like a continuous alarm.
"No greater lie has never been told"?:
A death alone could not save a dead -
One Live Soul....

To Lovers Too Stubborn

Two lovers too stubborn to pick up on their WRONG.
When shall the 2 become 1 and live like nothing but death....
WE ALL co-OWN?

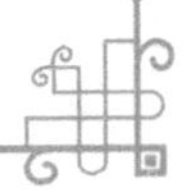

E-Y-E

I (eye) KNOWs WHO YOU BETTER NOT BE *FISHING* WITH

RUN UNTIL RUNNING RUNS OUT,
AND YOU WILL NEVER RUN AGAIN!
RUN UNTIL YOU WILL NEVER RUN AGAIN,
AND LOVE KNOWS NOT WHERE NOT TO FISH....

Dead Aches Or Rigor Mortis?

DIDN'T GOD USED TO LIVE HIGH UP THERE?
"THEY MOVED"!?
DIDN'T LOVE DYING MAKE DEATH UNFAIR?

Chick-N-Dump-Ns
(Baby, Give Mammas Daddies
Baby a One-Way-Kiss)

E(WE) (k)need(s) to get in that *kitchen/oven*,
Raise(rise) your children UP,
Put your *feat/feet* (see *"Act"*) DOWN,
And...along the *way*,
Change that weeping child's cloth -
diapers!!!

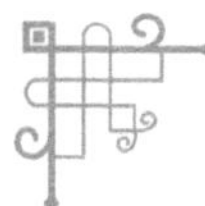

"Word"

EWE LEFT ME IN THE DARK/EYE LEFT EWE-N-(d) DUST
I LEFT YOU,
CAUSE LEAVING IS SUCH A MUST....

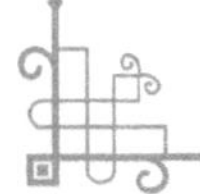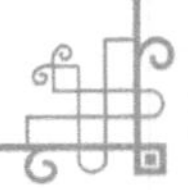

One More Than One
(Yo' Mamm y Is 2 Per Se Black)

There are two shades of *BLACK*,
And each is just as dark as the other...
If they weren't related,
Both of *these floods* could be Yo' "brother"!?

Bet Your Best Bet

I BET MY MAMMA AIN'T OLD! (now)....
Bet my daddy digs for gold (rush)...
Hell floods death like a roaring river preparing to un-flush....

Well-Wishers

(KISS MY SOUL 'TIL HEAVEN BECOMES UNDONE AGAIN)

IF I WANTED TO:
I COULD SMELL JUST LIKE I'M THE *NEXT HELL-RISEN-ROSE*,
BUT I'VE BEEN FREELY CROWNED FROM WEARING OUT MY
LOVE SHARPEST THORN.

IF I WANTED TO:
I COULD PIERCE MY SOUL TO LET MY BLUE BLOOD FLOOD
THE LONG, CIRCULAR ROAD,
IED RUN HELL ALL THE WAY TO HEAVEN...SMELL LIKE ALL
OVER-COOKED-OVER,
BUT HEAVEN SLEEPS ON SHEEP WHOSE LOT OF LIFE
BEFORE, DURING, AND PAST DAWN,
CAUSE LIFE IS ASLEEP, TRESPASSING ON THE LAMB...
PISSING ON HELL'S LAWN....

ECHO: AND DIE TO SEE HELL'S BURNT SUN....

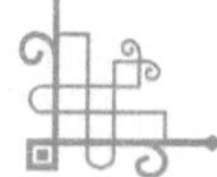

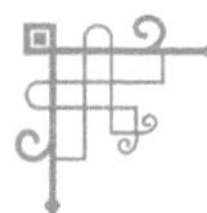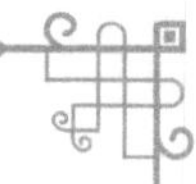

Mademoiselle

A damsel and a dame
Can make love take its *bilingual test.*
My cheat sheets, I do copy,
And answers my heart's request.

My damsel and mien francais goddess,
Call me by universel-translated names.
I scream to hear, "Oui, Monsieur,
Let's play a "itsy, bitsy" hand game.

Is my love being requite in kind,
For to dying my heart is not helped,
Penned under love's faux nom,
I am crushed by my *Coeur* deaths.

My love for my Jeune fille,
My heart's cardiac distress,
and my soul is at paradis paix,
watching this dame's armor undress.

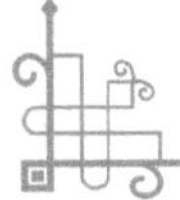

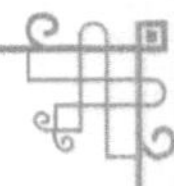

A Preferred or
Deferred Tally of Kisses

Unrequited love doesn't owe any admirable,
or even the courageous lover anything,
Except, maybe,
A fearless trip to the heavens,
Where true hearts are known to sail,
Forever,
Most Beautifully.

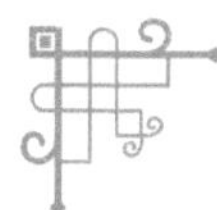

Untimiding the Ultimate
in Entertainment

The ultimate entertainment is being entertained,
Within the intertwining of your own.
(It is the redundancy that keeps love, anew).
Let's start over...
The ultimate intertrapment is to be the pardoned,
Who accused the imprisoned in the entrapped heart,
While setting out to sober a drunk morning dew.
Then permit me a trip in the trappings that encircle love,
Around a life that only interrupts to conjoin us two.

Lovesome

I'd kill for you,
And make you wash away my *sinister*,
Up, deep inside your dying, too.
For you,
I will chastise death,
On the eve of heaven's dawn.
I'll relieve God,
Let love thaw to a freezing, love-melt,
Then overthrow the self-inviting Sun.

Darkening-Darkness-Darker

I can entertain anybody's funny bullshit,
Even when it cuts so bullshittingly deep,
But, Please! Don't be kissing/bullshitting....
"M-E"!

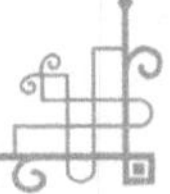

Something to Mull Over

Whenever you may shake your head from left to right,
Your head will still, eventually, swing from right to left.

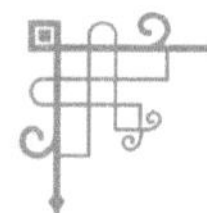
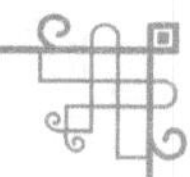

The Scolding, or "Why Couldn't You Have Taken Me with You"

"Can't take you all of the way with me,
Not to that place YOU might never go.
Because you people love Crucifixions,
Those previously persecuted do KNOW....

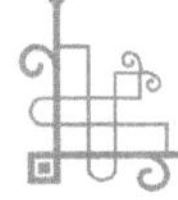

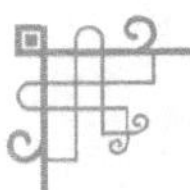
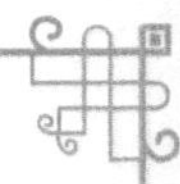

Neo-Timb er (or Piss off ")

And they called me a dog,
Unlike the tone of the one that is willing a winning title,
On the wretched, but free.
So, I told him, I said,
"Now this time you are barking up the right,
Unforgiving tree"!!!

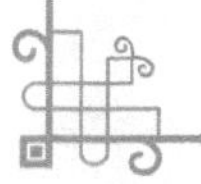

Medley (or "The Writer's Expanding Repertoire")

Two of my favorite songs are *"At last"* and *"Super Freak."*
These songs represent life's extraordinaries that
Are the prognostic fixation of Hope and Permissiveness....
Now, I can't wait to get my inheritance,
That patch of cemetery LOTS being manicured for *the meek.*
Because, *at last,* life will forever be chased by those
super-freakers....

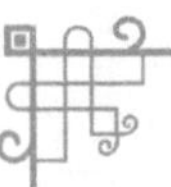

Love Fights Its Feelings

Love will throw a fight,
But only if love can win.
Love will start its FIGHT,
Just to fight the feelings...
Again!?

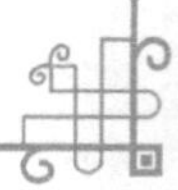

When I Wasn't Your Aging

When I wasn't your aging,
And you weren't that long ago,
Extrapolating on the fictional truth:
"Chickens are Niggers favorite cocks
To roost."

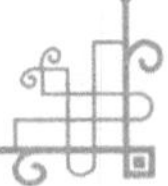

Table That Shit, Fool Sparrow Pig

I'd Like to Pawn Mister's Cash-Cow-Making-Swindling-
Swine for Some of Those Chitlins' (But, Don't
You Mix-Mind Without a Hog's Mauling)

I used to be able to tell a joke,
But cannot easily take over one now.
Now, one could only joke about being the little joker.
But when you are stuck between a pillar and stone,
Going "Uptown" or "Downtown"
If, unsexually,
The thrill of post bidding is gone.
What do you call with a overwhelming number of Spades,
As your wildest, of the once-played,
A cheater's card,
When you are pre-conditioned to shoot for the *heart*?!

That Truth is His Own Liar

I told my God mine truth,
But my black ass was not set the fuck free.
Because their light had dimmed so low,
The Creator could not make out
Who was lying *BEFORE Thee*....

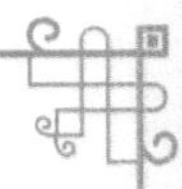

Keep Those Twin Souls in Procession

Keep those two souls in procession.
One is not the other,
Just its *badder* reflection.
Take those twin souls in succession.
The one time love kept being *fucked*,
Without any protection.

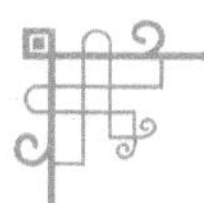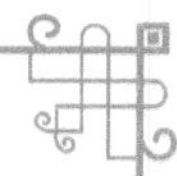

That Comedian's Comedian

If I am forced to laugh at my funny-loving-self,
Am I not still The Comedian?
If I misuse a little profanity-lacing,
Do I commit comedic sin?
If I am uplifted to sing a sightless song,
Under the holding of my breath,
Haven't I risen above my songless self?
If I shall pray:
Fuck the seed you brought forth n(WORD),"
Thief-Thieving-Thefter!
Am I not being sentenced,
For inhaling on *The Last of ONE Everlasting-Last-Breath?*

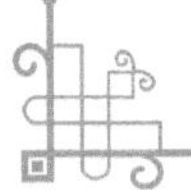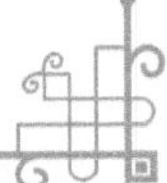

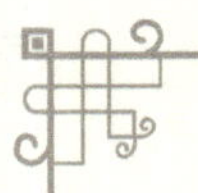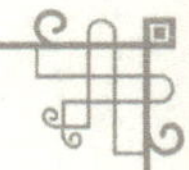

That is Why EYE/EWE Shouldn't Give (a fuck about) Directions

Wherever love travels that loving death follows!
(Who told God emptinesses aren't HOLLOWs)?
Who told everybody about LOVE's *Virgin* flight?
(Why did the *trustee thief* steal in the dark Night)?

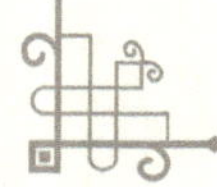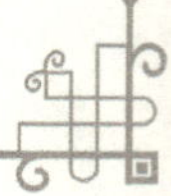

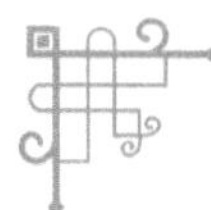

Too Blue for a Black Vote of Love

Love must never be taken lightly in light blue,
Even incomparable love pays an inflated price.
You might be forced to *purify* a *TAINTED* love...
TWICE!!!

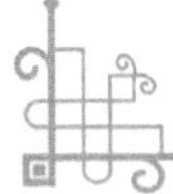

Conquest

If our hearts truly meet,
And LOVE is not a cheat.
Could it not be WRONG!?

If Love reaches LOVE's PEAK,
Walks away like LOVE's weak,
Isn't the VICTOR long GONE?

A Forgiveness to the Lovely

I awakened my God, This Day,
and just came right on out and then justifiably, begged:
"Freedom, what can't be reconciled,
Even when acquiescing with the same bitching,
between me and You?"
The Dead begged, fool,
Do unto him, with more forgiveness,
Exactly when the *Fool* has so lovingly *plagued* upon your Love.

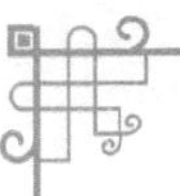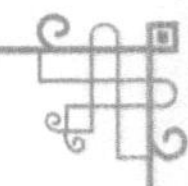

Thought I Smelled Something Burning

What are you doing burning - *Hear?*
"Thought I smelled something burning"!
Can you extinguish an inferno, *Dear?*
"I've spent my lifetimes in hell, learning."

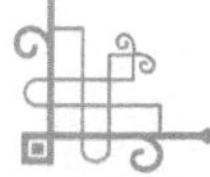

Dinner Date

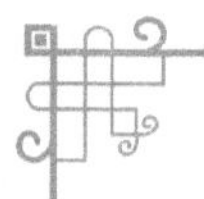
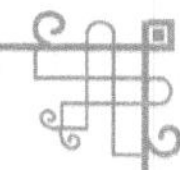

Love might die of hunger for love,
Or starve from its gluttonous hate.
Love is starving for its cooked dove;
The latter swoons on a dinner date.

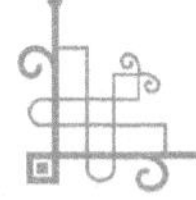

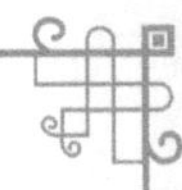

Tainted Gold

If the stars, ravishingly, impregnated the chastise moon,
Then lies with life but claiming to give the universe soul,
Who ages like fermented death soiling a path of tin gold,
That's too premature and living to be a postpartum, soon.

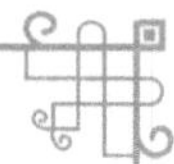

Just for the Taste of it

Did I sell my only soul to THAT devil?
If I did, what in the hell did I not buy!?
Check off "Old faith in the latest love,
As if the deceased tears never run dry.

I am on loan to the FIRST of MY lovers,
Who departed but cannot admit, "I left."
I am given his madness for purified hate,
This, I did buy, then split with owning self.

Thinking About Spanking EWE

Thank You," can have missed-interpretations,
Regarding the duration of welcoming one's overstay.
When I say "Thank You, Jesus"
You must know that I meant forthcoming of that assembly day.
When I say "Thank You," I was always never your friend,
Because you defended hate, until your mongering ends.

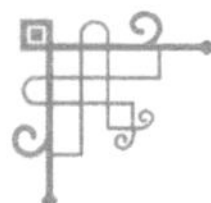

Posturing

Taken,
All of the earlier photographs,
When life gladly posed with its warm frown.
Because the late silhouettes are too dark and cold,
Even for the underground.

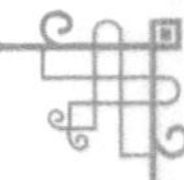

The Baker's Battle
(The Bottle Or "D" Bread)

When did manna's bread start producing molded crumbs?
What is the cost of batter to the bakery in the caked slum,
Whose tickets were punched for the gold-pavement street,
Whereby the *suns* do the baking and hell's carnage do eat.

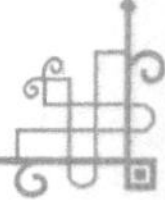

Aft er The Dead Lion Beat
The Sick Pig in a Raisie for Heaven

Death Have Assured The Mule That They Have *A LOT to Place*
(The next (neck) voice the you here (hear)
is that of THE-Ass's-Mule):
"Really? EWE ain't planning with US (Yo'
MAMA! Just Joking 2 Self)....
Without further DELAY....The ASS came in 1st! DISS EYE KNOW...
BUT, the real complicit, UNFORGIVING
niggers WERE KNOT the FOOLS
show....

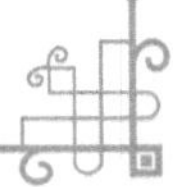

Compulsive

Taste it FIRST!? Taste it FIRST?!
Before adding a speck of that salt.
While pepper gleams in darkness,
Impulse is the fish that's CAUGHT!

Next to the Last Thing

The last thing on my mind is L-O-V-E.
Too much self-medicating gets in MY way.
I'll even think about living a little later,
On the anniversary of love's deferment day.

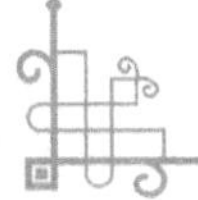

"Determined"

Determination dictates diction de decompression.
A lot of fucking "D" words just to get a curved-determined
"F" (fucked!).
"D" also is for "dichotomy."
These are the worries for today: "Dismay"
(a nigger-controlling conditional).
It also could represent "determined delinquent"
(needed and/ or in order).
Fancy shit for a Nigger who can't make the decision
of kicking ass with the shoe on or off.
And do you use a sock? Whose sock? Who washes
the shit stains? (your bad, not that hard).
By the way, are we talking about before you
walked in shit in search of the strings?
"D" stands for "distance."
That's what you will determine when you, if you
would, determine that his apology lost all
Value when he reinvented death-defying
(dead but loving me some dying).
My apologies to the new nigga who came late,
Cause these old niggers don't give a shit about "if" anymore.
To those honorees, "if" ain't nothing but a cause and an effect
(Scientific Negroes).
They are old schoolers, not that the school done fucked
around and the schooling gets older).
Since appropriate adjectives have not been reinvented (since
the beginning of your sentence),

Let's call the darker spades "black" ("light blue charcoaled").
This is somewhat intentional that they are called such
derogatory affections to reflect character (catering).
Cause you still demand that the "other" niggers
call the new niggers – "Negroes."
And I would not have it any different (for you).
But love tempers all. And love is why I stumble,
Then fall (stepping around love).
So, let's sum it up, all collectively together (look out for number 2).
Best yet, let's pretend like we are lovers that on occasion
might act true (after you got what they didn't want).
"Dismay!" (Trying to end it with a rhyme for us).
Dismay!"
Since the saints invented Easter,
The sinners determine the dietary restrictions of "Fatty
Tuesday" ("like gluttons prepared for
The (F)east....).

Echo:
Everything shall work out fine,
But that's determined by lying....
Not Time!!!.

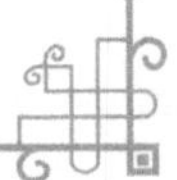

"Poetically Speaking"

Living to Bequeath my LOVE to Science,
This Liquid Life Forever a Leaking....
Let *Them curious scientists DETERMINE*
The CAUSES and The EFFECTS,
Scientifically Speaking.
Dying to save My salad from CAESAR,
That Tithe-Hill-Totin'-Leeching....
Them goddamn eternal revenuers can *KISS*
My FULLY-Delivered ASS,
UnApologetically Speaking.